Extreme Machines

eXtreme WATERCRAFT

IAN F. MAHANEY

PowerKiDS press
New York

Published in 2016 by
The Rosen Publishing Group, Inc.
29 East 21st Street, New York, NY 10010

Copyright © 2016 by The Rosen Publishing Group, Inc.

All rights reserved. No part of this book may be reproduced in any form without permission in writing from the publisher, except by a reviewer.

Developed and produced for Rosen by BlueAppleWorks Inc.

Art Director: T. J. Choleva
Managing Editor for BlueAppleWorks: Melissa McClellan
Designer: Greg Tucker
Photo Research: Jane Reid
Editor: Marcia Abramson

Photo Credits:
Cover Sunny Forest/Shutterstock; title page, 4 bottom, 16–17 Oleksandr Kalinichenko/Dreamstime; p. 4–5 U.S. Navy photo/Mass Communication Specialist 2nd Class Ryan D. McLearnon/Public Domain; p. 5 left SurangaSL/Shutterstock; p. 6 left Jocelyn Augustino/FEMA/Public Domain; p. 6–7 Fabio Formaggio/Dreamstime; p. 7 bottom Stephen Ausmus, USDA/Public Domain; p. 8 Yann Gwilhoù/Creative Commons; p. 9–10 Maxim Massalitin/Creative Commons; p. 10 bottom Gerd Fahrenhorst/Creative Commons; p. 10 top Clint Heuett/Public Domain; p. 11 top Crok Photography/Shutterstock; p. 11 Shaun Jeffers/Shutterstock; p. 12 left, 13 bottom Chuck Wagner/Shutterstock; p. 12–13 EvrenKalinbacak/Shutterstock;p/ 14–15 Federico Rostagno/Shutterstock; p. 15 top, 16 tcly/Shutterstock; p. 16 top Igor Karasi/Shutterstock; p. 17 top PA2 Dan Tremper, USCG/Public Domain; p. 17 right nui7711/Shutterstock; p. 18 left photomatz/Shutterstock; p. 18 Johann Ragnarsson/Dreamstime; p. 18–19 Wdeon/Dreamstime; p. 19 top Adrian Gilfillan/Dreamstime; p. 20 left Guillermo Colom, U.S. Coast Guard/Public Domain; p. 20–21 Eli Duke/Creative Commons; p. 21 bottom Wofratz/Creative Commons; p. 22 Ruth Peterkin/Dreamstime; p.23 left John Hedtke/Creative Commons; p. 23 middle Rennett Stowe/Creative Commons; p. 23 right Ozphotoguy/Shutterstock; p. 24 U.S. Navy photo/Public Domain; p. 24–25 U.S. Navy photo/Mass Communication Specialist 3rd Class Stephen D. Doyle II/Public Domain; p. 25 top U.S. Navy photo/Mass Communication Specialist 3rd Class Ricardo J. Reyes/Public Domain; p. 26 U.S. Navy photo/Photographer's Mate 2nd Class David C. Duncan/Public Domain; p. 26–27 U.S. Navy photo/PH1 Harold Gerwien/Public Domain; p. 27 top Bellona Foundation/Creative Commons; p. 28 DoD photo/Petty Officer 2nd Class Michael D. Degner, U.S. Navy/Public Domain; p. 28–29 U.S. Navy photo/Mass Communication Specialist 2nd Class Kristopher Wilson/Public Domain; p. 29 top U.S. Navy photo/Mass Communication Specialist Seaman Patrick Dionne/Public Domain.

Cataloging-in-Publication-Data
Mahaney, Ian F.
Extreme watercraft / by Ian F. Mahaney.
p. cm. — (Extreme machines)
Includes index.
ISBN 978-1-4994-1191-1 (pbk.)
ISBN 978-1-4994-1220-8 (6 pack)
ISBN 978-1-4994-1229-1 (library binding)
1. Ships — Juvenile literature. 2. Boats and boating — Juvenile literature.
3. Personal watercraft — Juvenile literature. 4. Tankers — Juvenile literature.
I. Mahaney, Ian F. II. Title.
VM150.M3484 2016
623.8—d23

Manufactured in the United States of America
CPSIA Compliance Information: Batch #WS15PK: For Further Information contact: Rosen Publishing, New York, New York at 1-800-237-9932

Contents

What Is a Watercraft?	4
EXTREME PROPULSION	
Extreme Air-Powered Boats	6
Extreme Solar-Powered Boats	8
Extreme Jet-Powered Boats	10
Lightning Speed	12
EXTREME OCEAN LINERS	
Giant Freighters	14
Massive Oil Tankers	16
Fish-Processing Factories	18
Extreme Pathfinders	20
Cruising in Style	22
IN THE MILITARY	
Floating Airports	24
Underwater Fortresses	26
Multitasking Hovercrafts	28
GLOSSARY	30
FOR MORE INFORMATION	31
INDEX	32

What Is a Watercraft?

Water covers more than 70% of Earth. A watercraft is a vessel that travels on or in the water. There are many types of watercraft. Most watercraft float on the water's surface. These vehicles can float because the **volume** of water beneath the watercraft weighs the same as the watercraft. Ships, boats, **kayaks**, and canoes are watercraft that float. These watercraft also have hollow areas filled with air or lightweight materials. This helps watercraft float.

LNG carriers transport liquefied natural gas in large tanks. These ships have a double bottom and many high-tech safety devices.

4

Water Travel

Humans made the first watercraft thousands of years ago. They rode on floating logs. Soon people dug wood out of the logs so they had a place to sit while riding in their watercraft.

This book is about the biggest and fastest watercraft. This book includes boats, ships, submarines, and other extreme watercraft that explore all areas of Earth's lakes, rivers, and oceans. Extreme watercraft can do a lot of work. They move heavy loads of oil around the globe. Extreme watercraft can also carry people on the ocean for vacations or race across lakes for fun.

One aircraft carrier serves as a floating base for dozens of military planes and helicopters.

Motorboats come in all sizes, from one-person models all the way to giant **yachts**.

EXTREME PROPULSION

Extreme Air-Powered Boats

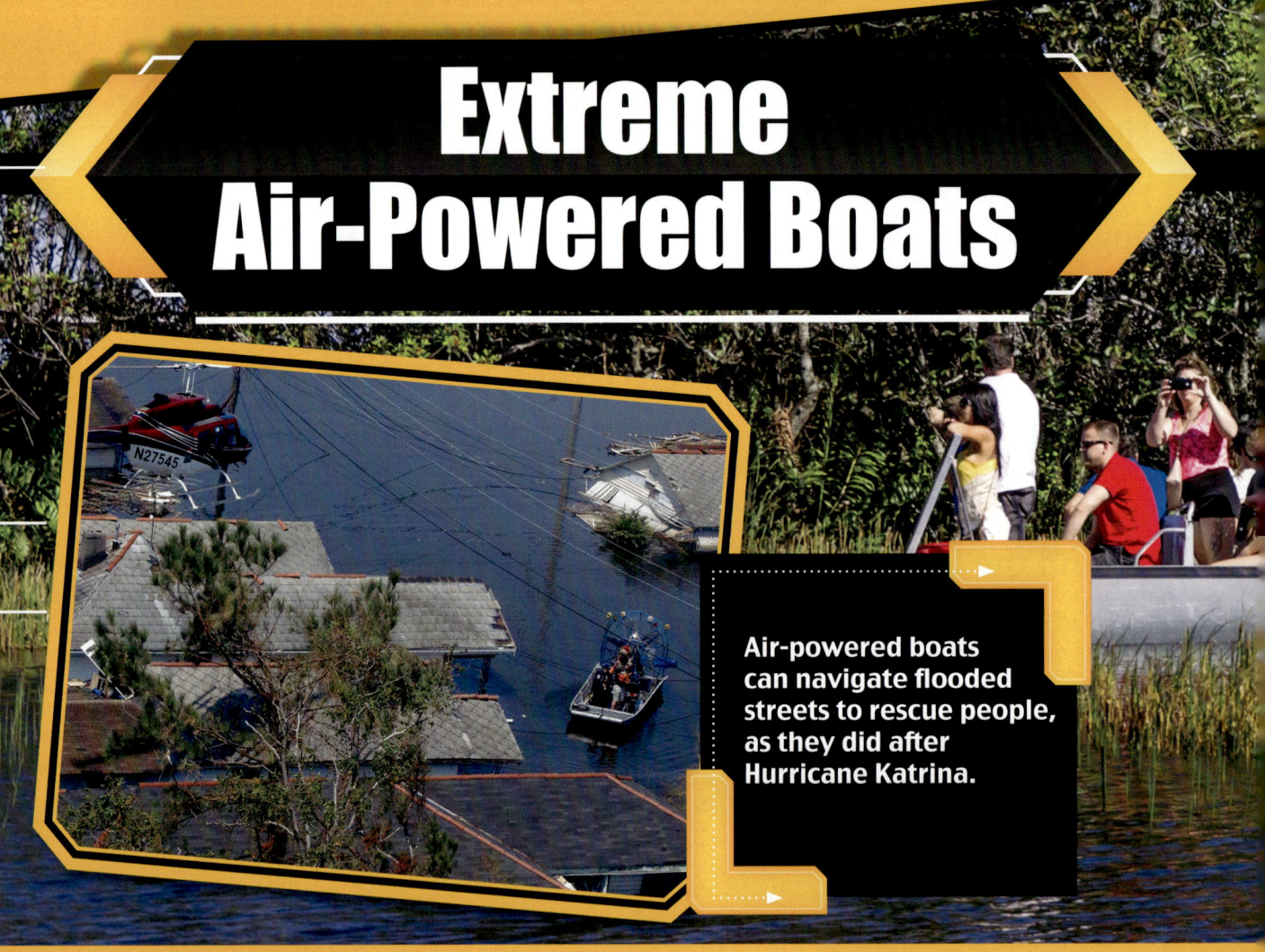

Air-powered boats can navigate flooded streets to rescue people, as they did after Hurricane Katrina.

Motorboats are boats with engines. **Propellers** power most motorboats. Propellers are made from metal or other hard materials. They hang in the water and are very powerful, but propellers require deep water free from rocks to work.

Many people use airboats to **navigate** difficult **terrain**. People use them to go hunting and fishing. People also race airboats. They can speed at more than 100 miles (160 km) per hour. Private companies also take tourists on trips to see wildlife such as snakes and alligators. The biggest airboats can hold 24 passengers.

Did You Know?

Airboats are fun to ride, but they are not just for tourists. With their flat bottoms, they are ideal for rescue operations in shallow water, during floods, and even on ice. When Hurricane Katrina hit New Orleans in 2005, airboats came from all over the country to help with search and rescue.

Scientists also use airboats. They travel into shallow water to collect samples.

Shallow Watercraft

In shallow water, fans power some boats. These boats are called airboats or fanboats. These small watercraft are designed to travel over shallow, wet surfaces. They can ride on shallow rivers, over marshes, and through swamps. Some airboats can even drive on land.

Fanboats are popular in Florida and other areas with shallow water. These watercraft are normally between 6 feet (1.8 m) and 30 feet (9 m) long, and they have a fan on the back that **propels** them through the water. An aircraft or automobile engine runs the fan on the back. People often use automobile engines because it is easy to find replacement parts when an airboat needs repair.

Extreme Solar-Powered Boats

Many boats and ships use fuel such as **diesel** or gasoline to power their travel. Other boats and ships have sails on their masts. These sails use the wind's energy to power the watercraft. Still other watercraft have electric motors.

Solar-powered boats are extreme electric boats. The biggest solar-powered boat is called the *Tûranor PlanetSolar*. It is about 115 feet (35 m) long, 75 feet (23 m) wide, and weighs almost 100 tons (90 metric tons).

The *Tûranor* is a **catamaran**. A catamaran is a watercraft with two hulls. These hulls keep a boat afloat and a catamaran has a platform that connects the hulls.

Solar panels work best when clean. On a boat, they must be cleared regularly of plant matter, dirt, and bird droppings.

Did You Know?

Solar power turns the energy of sunlight into electricity. The sunlight is collected on glass-like panels made of silicon, a material found in sand.

The *Tûranor* continues to be an ambassador for renewable energy, hosting public tours and private events.

Around the World

The *Tûranor* has been used for climate research and to study the ocean. This watercraft has traveled all over the world. A German company built the vessel and finished construction in 2010. Since then the watercraft has sailed across the Atlantic Ocean. The *Tûranor PlanetSolar* also was the first solar-powered watercraft to **circumnavigate**, or travel all the way around, the Earth. It traveled more than 32,000 nautical miles. A nautical mile is a unit of measure used in sea travel. Nautical miles measure distance and Earth's shape. One nautical mile equals about 1.15 miles or 1.85 km.

Extreme Jet-Powered Boats

Like fanboats, jet boats can speed through shallow water. A New Zealander named Bill Hamilton invented jet boats in the 1950s. Hamilton liked spending time outdoors and he wanted to ride in boats on the shallow rivers of New Zealand. Like fanboats, jet boats can avoid rocks on the bottom of a river because they do not drop a propeller into the water. Jet boats move by shooting water through their extreme engine and out the back end. Hamilton's jet boats were made of wood. Today's jet boats are often made of metal. These metal jet boats can ride on shallow water, but they can also ride on rivers with rocks. In fact, companies take tourists on speedy jet boat tours of rivers that have rocks and whitewater rapids. These watercraft can cruise at more than 40 miles (64 km) per hour.

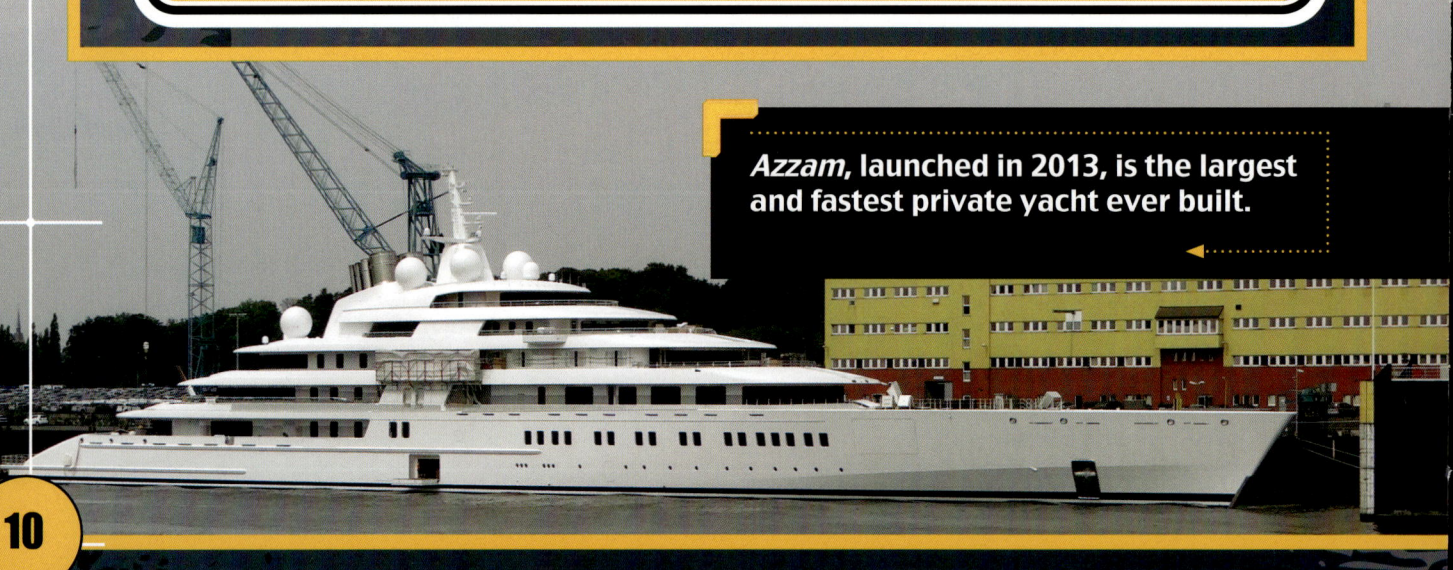

Azzam, launched in 2013, is the largest and fastest private yacht ever built.

Speed Record

Personal watercraft are the smallest jet boats. They can carry up to three people and the fastest personal watercraft can reach speeds of 80 miles (129 km) per hour.

Riders stand or sit on a personal watercraft. There is no opening for an inside seat.

Jet boats take tourists on thrill rides in New Zealand (left) and all over the world.

Powerful Jets

Jet boats come in sizes from small to huge. The largest jet boats are ferries and yachts. They often travel in deeper water. One luxury yacht called the *Azzam* is 590 feet (180 m) long and has four jets on the back that propel the watercraft forward at more than 30 miles (48 km) per hour.

Lightning Speed

People race all kinds of watercraft. People race kayaks and canoes. They race personal watercraft and sailboats. Sailboats compete in races around the world. Some sailboat races are even races around the whole world. Clipper Round the World is a race around the world. It is 40,000 nautical miles long.

Powerboats are some of the fastest watercraft that people race. Powerboats are motorboats especially made for racing. These boats are long, narrow, and very powerful. Powerboats are so fast that their **bows** lift off the water when they race. Offshore powerboat racing is popular in the United States and other countries. In these competitions, powerboats race around a water track. Sometimes these races are longer than 200 miles (320 km).

Powerboats have a streamlined hull, which improves their speed and handling.

Making a Splash

The Miss Geico racing team drives catamarans in Offshore Powerboat Racing. These extreme watercraft normally have two crew members and some Miss Geico powerboats can race faster than 200 miles (320 km) per hour.

Drag boat racing is an even faster form of motorboat racing. In drag boat racing, two drivers compete in a short race that is a straight line. Drag racing boats can speed along faster than 250 miles (400 km) per hour.

Did You Know?

Ken Warby of Australia set a world record in 1978. He drove his boat, the *Spirit of Australia*, at more than 315 miles (507 km) per hour. That's the fastest anyone has ever traveled in a boat.

Dual-hulled power catamarans can achieve faster speeds than single-hulled powerboats.

EXTREME OCEAN LINERS

Giant Freighters

More than half of the world's international trade gets to its destination on cargo ships.

Container ships are huge watercraft used to haul cargo around the world. They haul many types of cargo from food to electronics to cars. These ships carry containers that are waterproof metal boxes. The boxes can be different **dimensions**. The unit used to measure these containers is called the twenty-foot equivalent unit or TEU. One TEU is 20 feet (6 m) long. The height and width of these containers vary, but often 1 TEU is 8 feet (2.4 m) wide and 8 feet 6 inches (2.6 m) tall. Each container measuring 1 TEU can fit about two cars.

The truck-size containers are loaded onto semis or trains after the ship docks.

Oversized Triple Es

Triple Es haul cargo between Asia and Europe. There are no ports in the United States that can handle ships that big. Triple Es are also too big to fit through the Panama Canal.

Oceangoing Giants

Shipping companies used the first container ships in the 1950s. These container ships could hold between 500 and 800 containers. Another way to say this is that these ships could carry between 500 and 800 TEU.

Today's container ships are huge. The biggest container ships are called the Maersk Lines Triple Es. The *Mærsk Mc-Kinney Møller* is one Triple E container ship. Triple Es are 1,312 feet (400 m) long and 194 feet (59 m) wide. They can carry 18,000 TEU. That's 36,000 cars!

Each Triple E has two propellers that power the ship through the water. Each propeller is more than 30 feet (9 m) wide.

Massive Oil Tankers

Supertankers are huge ships used to transport oil. Many of these ships are so big that they sail close to a port, but they can't dock at the port. They stay at sea and unload their load of oil into pipes that carry the oil to land. The longest ship ever built was a supertanker. It was called the *Seawise Giant* and was more than 1,500 feet (457 m) long. Today, T1 supertankers are the biggest supertankers. The T1s can also carry more oil than any other tanker in the world.

Supertankers often pick up cargo at offshore platforms where oil can be pumped aboard through hoses. Ship-to-ship transfer also may be used.

The *Hellespont Alhambra* was one of the largest supertankers. It has been renamed the *T1 Asia* and serves as a floating storage and offloading facility.

When supertankers spill or leak oil, the environment can be seriously damaged.

Sticky Cargo

The weight a ship can carry is called its deadweight tonnage or DWT. The DWT is the maximum amount of cargo and fuel the supertanker can haul without sinking too far in the water or reaching the bottom of small passageways such as canals. The DWT for T1 supertankers includes the oil the tankers can transport. A T1 supertanker can carry more than 3 million barrels of oil. One barrel of oil equals 42 gallons (159 L) and weighs about 300 pounds (136 kg). This means a T1 supertanker can carry more than 900 million pounds (408 million kg) of oil. This much oil weighs more than 2,000 blue whales.

Fish-Processing Factories

Boats around the world search for fish. They fish on lines and with nets. Some fishing boats are small. Other fishing boats are huge. Many commercial fishing boats are trawlers. Trawlers are boats that drag nets to catch fish. Trawlers often haul their catch back to shore where workers freeze or can the fish. Workers also ship fresh fish to supermarkets.

Other huge fishing boats and ships catch fish then freeze or can the fish onboard. These boats employ fishermen who spend weeks at a time at sea. These boats catch huge amounts of fish such as Alaskan pollock and tuna. Boats that freeze or can their own fish are often called floating fish factories or floating fish-processing factories.

Trawlers can be big or small. Many large trawlers carry some basic fish-processing equipment. Smaller trawlers keep fish on ice until they get to shore.

Smaller fishing operations use traditional land-based processing plants.

The *Nisshin Maru* does all the processing for Japan's seven-ship whaling fleet. It is also used for conducting research.

Power Fishing

The biggest floating fish factory is called the *Lafayette* floating fish-processing factory. It serves as a mothership for a fleet of fishing vessels. The catches of these vessels are transported on board *Lafayette* where they are sorted, processed, and frozen. Final fish products are then picked up by transporter ships and sent directly to markets. The *Lafayette* is a converted oil tanker that is more than 945 feet (288 m) long. It weighs 50,000 tons (45,400 metric tons). If operated year round, this fishing factory could process and freeze more than 600,000 tons (544,300 metric tons) of fish.

Extreme Pathfinders

The U.S. Coast Guard uses small icebreakers in the Great Lakes (left) and big ones at the Poles.

Icebreakers are awesome watercraft, with powerful engines, that are heavy enough to break and crush ice. These extreme vehicles clear a path to deliver cargo or break the ice so a second ship can transport fuel or other freight. Countries such as the United States, Canada, and Russia keep icebreakers for missions that deliver supplies to **civilians** and research stations near the North and South Poles. The U.S. Coast Guard keeps Polar Class icebreakers for these missions. These icebreakers are almost 400 feet (122 m) long, 80 feet (24 m) wide, and they can carry 400 tons (363 metric tons) of cargo. Icebreakers have strong hulls that cut through ice. Icebreakers can also lift their bows onto the ice and crush it. Polar Class icebreakers can break through ice that's more than 20 feet (6 m) thick.

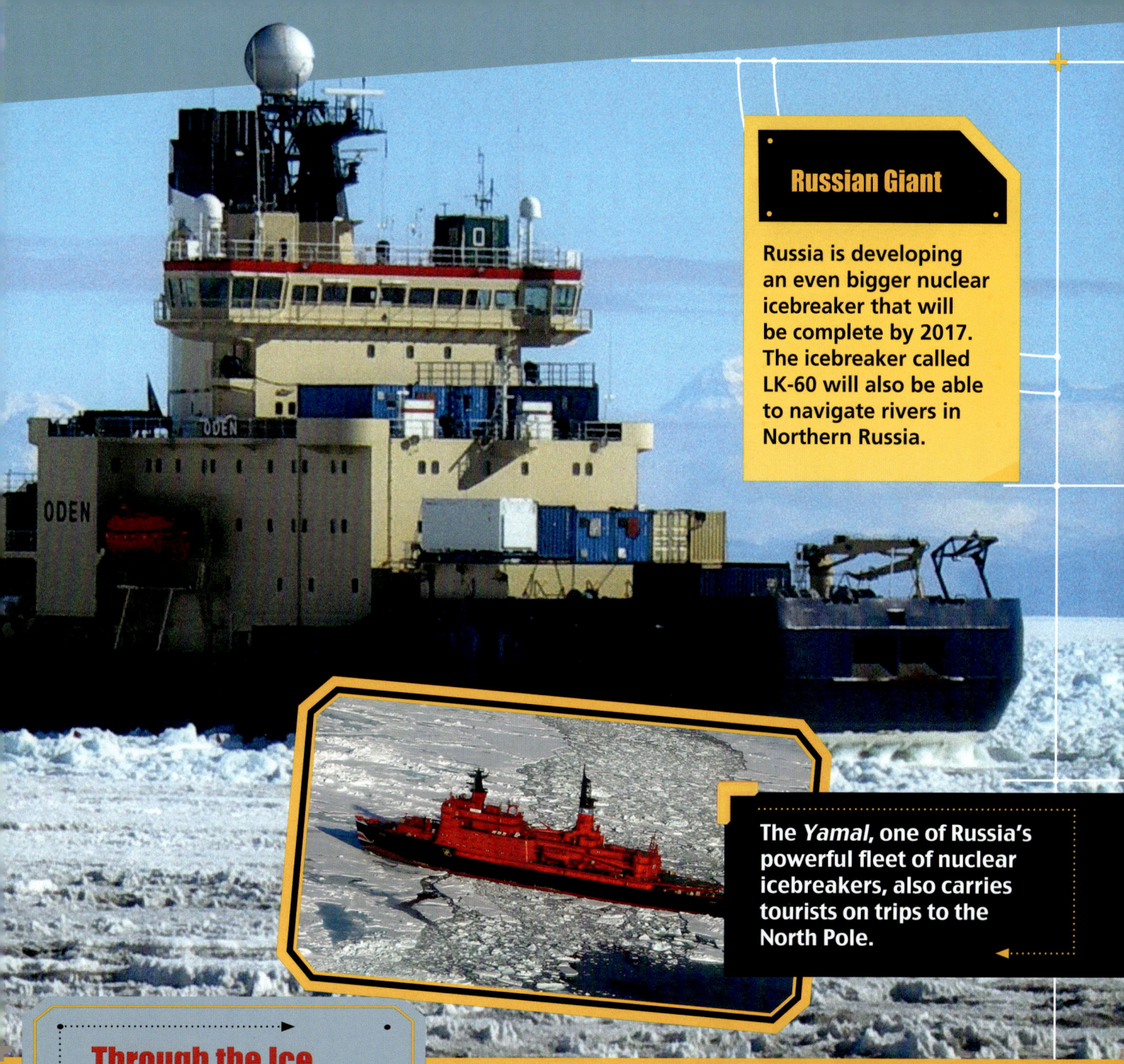

Russian Giant

Russia is developing an even bigger nuclear icebreaker that will be complete by 2017. The icebreaker called LK-60 will also be able to navigate rivers in Northern Russia.

The *Yamal*, one of Russia's powerful fleet of nuclear icebreakers, also carries tourists on trips to the North Pole.

Through the Ice

Polar Class icebreakers are diesel-powered icebreakers. Russia uses diesel icebreakers, but Russia also has **nuclear**-powered icebreakers. Nuclear-powered icebreakers are powerful and break ice for years before they need to be refueled. The largest icebreaker in the world is a Russian nuclear icebreaker called the *NS 50 Let Pobedy*. It can crush ice 9 feet (2.7 m) thick and run for years, longer than any diesel icebreaker.

Cruising in Style

Cruise ships are amazing watercraft. They are huge vessels that take people for vacation on the ocean.

Some cruise ships are huge. The *Allure of the Seas* is the biggest cruise ship ever made. It is 1,187 feet (362 m) long and 213 feet (65 m) wide. That's more than three times the area of an NFL football field.

The *Allure of the Seas* has three propellers that are each 20 feet (6 m) wide. These propellers drive the cruise ship at 22.6 knots when sailing the seas. A knot is a unit of measure used for sea travel. One knot equals one nautical mile per hour. One knot equals about 1.15 miles (1.85 km) per hour.

Popular cruise stops such as the Caribbean and Hawaiian islands can get very crowded.

Floating Hotels

Like other cruise ships, the *Allure of the Seas* has many entertainment options. This cruise ship has four swimming pools and 10 whirlpools. The watercraft has a movie theater, a miniature golf course, a rock climbing wall, and an ice-skating rink. The cruise ship has a zip line that passengers can ride down nine levels or decks. In total, the watercraft has 16 decks and 2,704 rooms. More than 6,000 passengers can ride on the cruise ship and the ship has about 2,700 crew members.

Did You Know?

The *Allure of the Seas* has a sister ship called the *Oasis of the Seas*. They were supposed to be the same size, but when they were complete, *Allure* was two inches (5 cm) longer than *Oasis*.

With so much to do on board, some passengers never leave the ship during their cruise.

IN THE MILITARY

Floating Airports

The first nuclear aircraft carrier, the USS *Enterprise*, served for more than 50 years before being retired.

Aircraft carriers are huge watercraft that navies around the world use as main battleships. Aircraft carriers are floating airports that can transport fighter planes anywhere on Earth's oceans.

Aircraft carriers have very short runways. The carriers have **catapults** that propel the aircraft to takeoff. Planes catch a cable onboard the aircraft carriers when the planes land.

The United States has 10 Nimitz class aircraft carriers. Nuclear power fuels these watercraft. Nimitz aircraft carriers are 1,092 feet (333 m) long and 252 feet (77 m) wide. That's longer than the height of the Eiffel Tower. The Eiffel Tower is 986 feet (300 m) tall.

Aircraft carriers changed the nature of warfare forever by allowing planes to operate without a base on land.

Moving Runways

Nimitz class aircraft carriers hold at least 60 aircraft. These planes take off and land on runways that are 320 feet (98 m) long.

The U.S. Navy is building new aircraft carriers called Gerald Ford class aircraft carriers. These aircraft carriers are named after the 38th president of the United States. Gerald Ford aircraft carriers will replace the Nimitz class aircraft carriers. The new aircraft carriers are about the same dimensions as Nimitz class aircraft carriers, but the new aircraft carriers will carry more airplanes. Gerald Ford class aircraft carriers will carry at least 75 aircraft.

25

Underwater Fortresses

Submarines are watercraft that can float on the water's surface or dive into the ocean to hide. These watercraft have tanks called **ballast** tanks that are filled with either air or water. When a sub's ballast tanks are filled with air the sub floats. When the ballast tanks are filled with water the sub dives into the ocean.

Today's submarines are incredible. Many submarines run on nuclear power. These subs can stay at sea or even underwater for months at a time. Many navies around the world use submarines. Countries such as China and the United States have submarines.

When it is necessary, submarines can surface very quickly.

Typhoon Class Submarines

Russia has the largest subs in the world. They are called the Typhoon class. These subs are 574 feet (175 m) long and carry 20 long-range missiles.

Typhoons and other military subs are painted black for **camouflage**.

Getting into port is a team effort for a large nuclear sub. A smaller boat usually is assigned to assist.

Powerful and Dangerous

The United States has several kinds of submarines. The U.S. Navy has subs called fast attack submarines. They defend and possibly attack enemy targets with **torpedoes** and missiles. The United States also has large submarines that carry torpedoes and missiles. These larger subs can travel long distances.

The United States' Ohio class submarines are enormous. They are 560 feet (171 m) long and 155 sailors ride aboard as the crew. Ohio class subs can steam along faster than 20 knots and the subs carry long-range missiles. The U.S. Navy has 14 Ohio class submarines and each sub can carry 24 Trident 2 missiles.

Multitasking Hovercrafts

Hovercrafts are watercraft that float above the water. These vehicles create an area of high pressure beneath the vehicle that keeps the watercraft elevated. Hovercrafts also have rubber skirts around the vehicles that contain the areas of high pressure.

People all over the world use hovercrafts. Civilians use these watercraft for races and ferries. People also use hovercrafts to cruise on the water for fun. The fastest driver once drove a hovercraft faster than 85 miles (137 km) per hour.

Military forces throughout the world use hovercraft. The Russian ZUBR class of hovercrafts are the world's largest hovercrafts. These vehicles are 187 feet (57 m) long, and can carry 500 troops or 130 tons (118 metric tons) of cargo.

The military uses powerful hovercrafts to carry people, equipment, trucks, and even tanks across water.

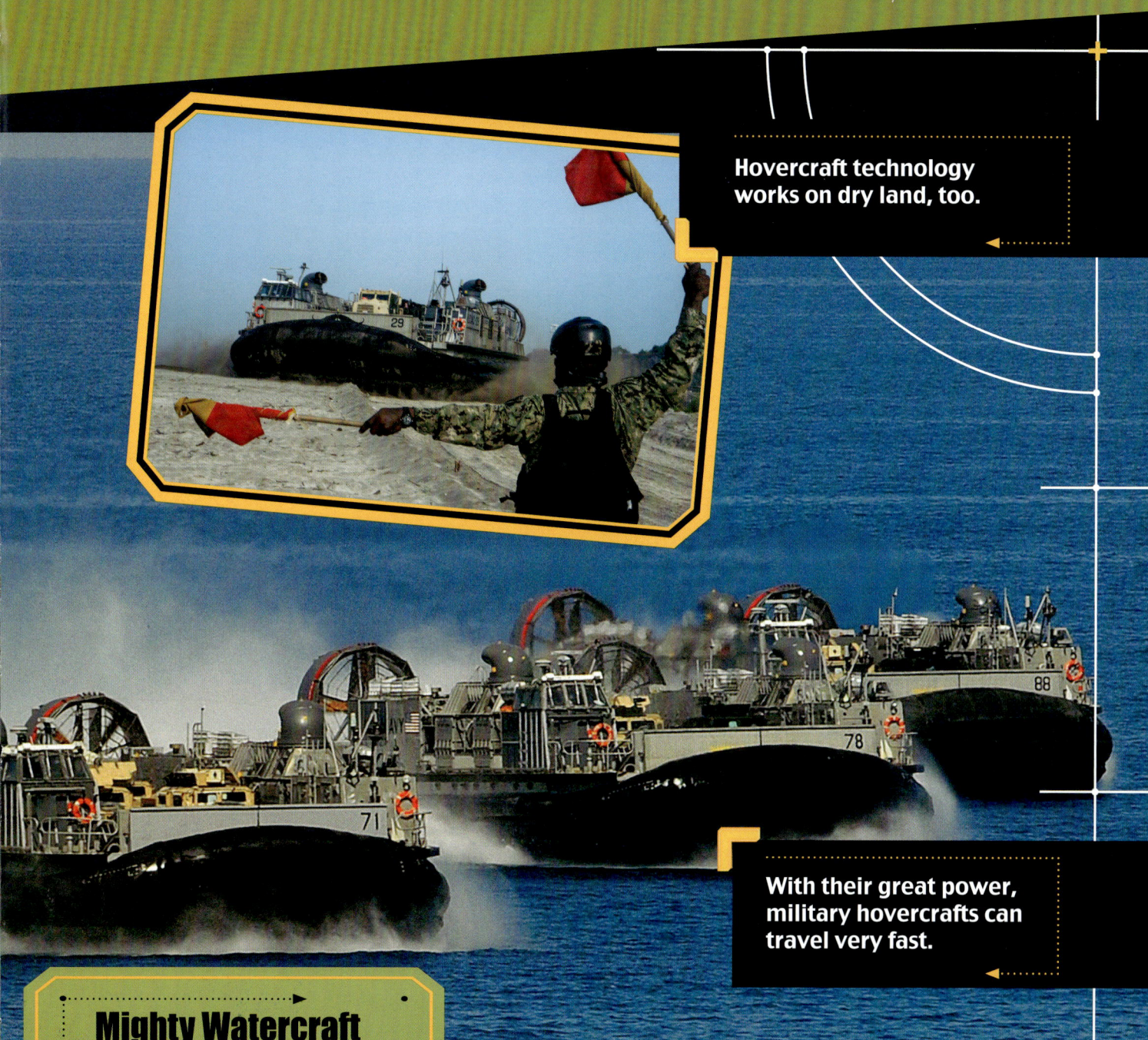

Hovercraft technology works on dry land, too.

With their great power, military hovercrafts can travel very fast.

Mighty Watercraft

The U.S. Navy uses hovercraft to transport troops, ships, and vehicles. The Navy's LCAC (Landing Craft Air Cushion) hovercraft is 81 feet (25 m) long and can haul a tank.

Hovercrafts are extreme watercraft. There are many other extreme watercraft, too. Some watercraft carry a lot of cargo. Other watercraft are the speediest vehicles on the water. These extreme watercraft from submarines to racing boats to supertankers help civilians, companies, and the military do a lot of work every day.

GLOSSARY

ballast A heavy material that is used to make something steady, especially a ship.

bows The front part of boats and ships.

camouflage A way of hiding something by making it match its surroundings.

catamaran A vessel, usually propelled by sail, that has two hulls or floats held side by side by a frame above them.

catapult A device built to launch something into the air.

circumnavigate To sail all the way around.

civilians People who are not in the military.

diesel A type of liquid fuel that is an alternative to gasoline.

dimensions The length, width, or height of an object.

hulls The frames or bodies of ships.

kayak A small, lightweight boat that is shaped like a canoe, covered on top, and powered by oars.

navigate To steer on a route.

nuclear Having to do with or based on the energy in the nucleus, or core, of an atom.

propellers Mechanical devices for propelling a boat or aircraft, which include a shaft with two or more angled blades attached to it.

propels Pushes or drives something in a particular direction.

terrain The physical qualities of a piece of land.

torpedoes Exploding weapons that are shaped like a cylinder.

volume The amount of space that matter takes up.

yachts Large watercraft generally used for pleasure.

FOR MORE INFORMATION

Further Reading

Frith, Alex. *Submarines.*
London, UK: Usborne Books, 2011.

Gigliotti, Jim. *Powerboat Racing.*
North Mankato, MN: The Child's World, 2012.

Harasymiw, Mark. *Life on a Submarine.*
New York, NY: Gareth Stevens Publishing, 2013.

Parker, Steve. *Ships and Submarines.*
Broomall, PA: Mason Crest Publishers, 2011.

Scheff, Matt. *Hovercraft.*
Edina, MN: ABDO Publishing, 2015.

Sobey, Ed. *The Motorboat Book: Build & Launch 20 Jet Boats, Paddle-Wheelers, Electric Submarines & More.*
Chicago, IL: Chicago Review Press, 2013.

Websites

Due to the changing nature of Internet links, PowerKids Press has developed an online list of websites related to the subject of this book. This site is updated regularly. Please use this link to access the list:
www.powerkidslinks.com/em/water

INDEX

A
airboats 6, 7
aircraft carriers 5, 24, 25
Allure of the Seas 22, 23
Azzam 10, 11

B
boats 4, 5, 6, 7, 8, 10, 11, 12, 13, 18, 29

C
catamaran(s) 8, 13
container ships 14
cruise ships 22

F
fanboats 7
ferries 11, 28
float 4, 26, 28
floating fish-processing factories 18

H
Hellespont Alhambra 17
hovercrafts 28, 29

I
icebreakers 20

J
jet boats 10, 11

L
Lafayette 19
LNG carriers 4

M
Mærsk Mc-Kinney Møller 15
motorboats 5, 6

N
Nisshin Maru 19
NS 50 Let Pobedy 21
nuclear power 24

O
Oasis of the Seas 23

P
personal watercraft 11, 12
Polar Class icebreakers 20, 21
powerboats 12

S
sails 8
Seawise Giant 16
ships 4, 5, 8, 14, 15, 16, 18, 22, 23, 29
solar-powered boats 8
Spirit of Australia 13
submarines 5, 26, 27, 29
supertankers 16

T
trawlers 18
Tûranor PlanetSolar 8, 9

U
U.S. Navy 25, 27, 29

Y
yachts 5, 11
Yamal 21

32